MY MOM'S O·K·A·Y

·A·MUDPIE ™ ·STORY·
·straight·to·you·from·
·KITT'NVILLE·BY·
GUY GILCHRIST

CHECKERBOARD ☆ PRESS ☆

NEW YORK·NEW YORK

My name is Mudpie. This is a story all about me and my mom.

One morning I woke up early and got dressed. I wanted to make breakfast for my mom, because my mom's okay.

You should have seen
how SURPRISED she was!

Then I helped my mom do the laundry. I put in lots of extra soap to get the clothes extra clean. I did that part all by myself.

But my mom helped me clean up the bubbles.

We go for rides in my mom's car.

Sometimes my mom rides in my car . . . but not too often.

One day I painted a picture for my mom.

She LOVED it! My mom's okay.

One day I went out in my backyard to pick some flowers for my mom.

But the bumbley-bees picked on me!

My mom didn't get the flowers. I got a Band-Aid.

So I went and got her ANOTHER present.

But this present ran away! My mom said, "Thank you anyway, Mudpie. It's the thought that counts."

Well, if it's the thought that counts, I think that my mom's okay in a thousand ways every day.